OLD
WOOD
BOAT

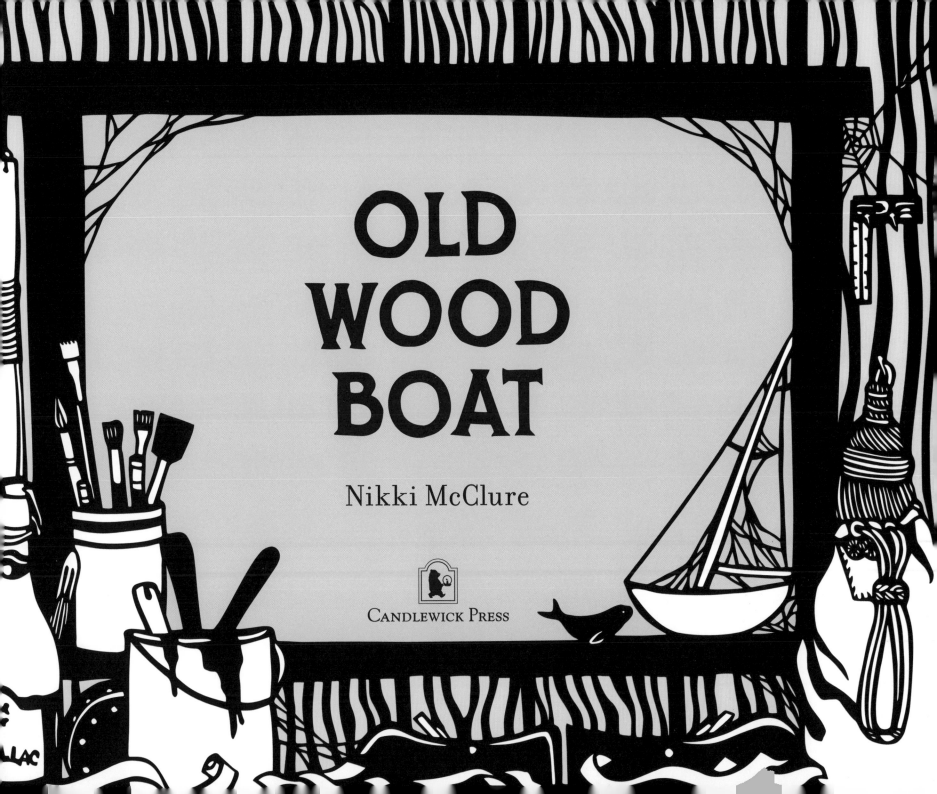

OLD WOOD BOAT

Nikki McClure

CANDLEWICK PRESS

Old Wood Boat sits in the yard.

She remembers the wind.

She remembers islands and a sea of green.

She remembers and she waits.

Rain seeps in.

The sun dries her.

She cracks. And she waits.

Blackberries creep across her decks,

and raccoons lounge below.

And still she waits, softening, oldening.

Then one day, a family arrives.

They peek and poke and climb up high.

They love Old Wood Boat.

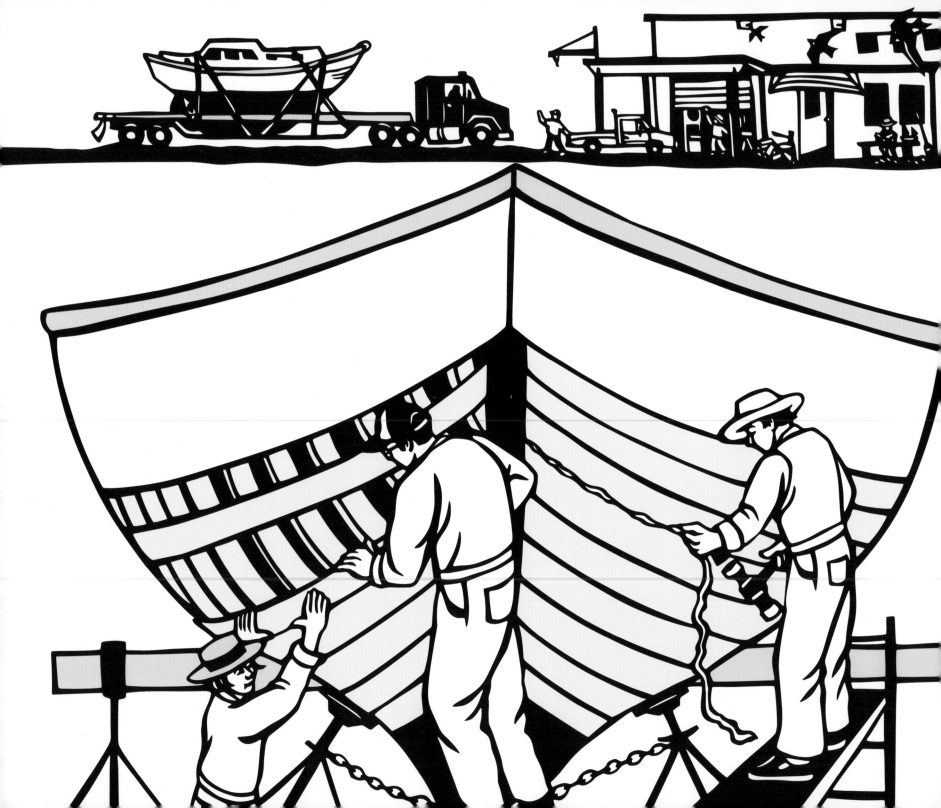

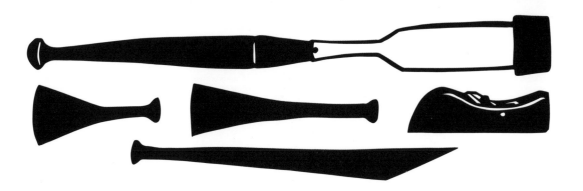

They tow her home, scrape and scrub.

They fit new planks, caulk her seams to make her watertight and strong.

They sand and varnish her until she shines.

They mend her sails to hold the wind and tighten her
shrouds for when the wind blows a gale.
They sew new cushions for the berths below
and hang bright yellow curtains in the galley.

Old Wood Boat is beautiful again.

They lower her into the water.

Will she float?

Will she sink?

She rocks and bobs in the cold water,
and her sides sparkle with light.
She floats! Three cheers!

Her family steps aboard, and they feel her come alive.

Her flags flap. They pour libations to every sea spirit they know.

Old Wood Boat floats on the little green sea with her new family.

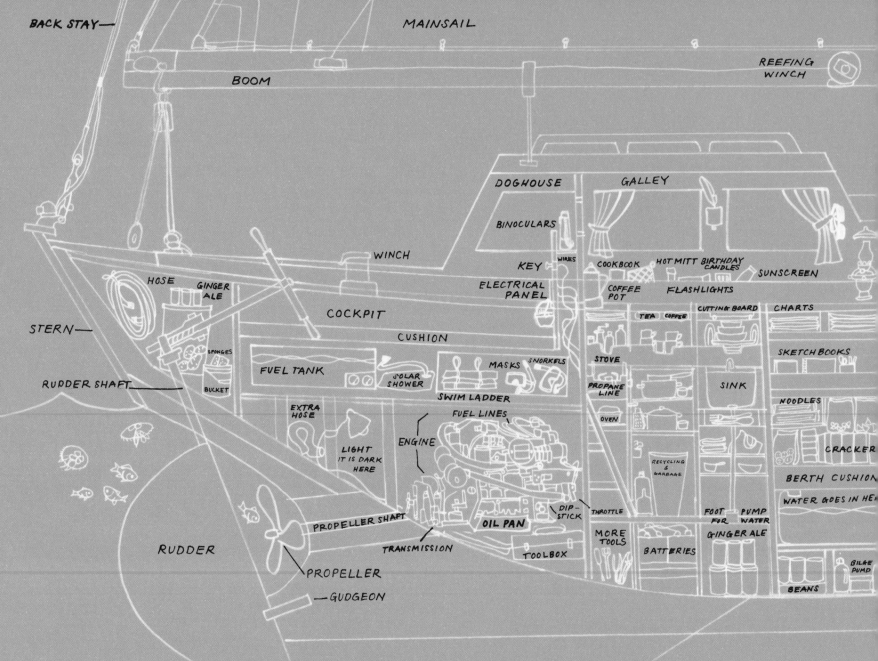

BACK STAY—

MAINSAIL

REEFING WINCH

BOOM

DOGHOUSE   GALLEY

BINOCULARS

HOSE   GINGER ALE

WINCH

KEY

ELECTRICAL PANEL

COCKPIT

STERN—

CUSHION

RUDDER SHAFT

SPONGES

BUCKET

FUEL TANK

SOLAR SHOWER

SWIM LADDER

MASKS   SNORKELS

STOVE

PROPANE LINE

OVEN

EXTRA HOSE

ENGINE

FUEL LINES

LIGHT IT IS DARK HERE

RECYCLING & GARBAGE

PROPELLER SHAFT

OIL PAN

DIP-STICK   THROTTLE

RUDDER

TRANSMISSION

TOOLBOX

MORE TOOLS

BATTERIES

FOOT FOR   PUMP WATER

GINGER ALE

PROPELLER

—GUDGEON

WIRES   COOKBOOK   HOT MITT BIRTHDAY CANDLES   SUNSCREEN

COFFEE POT   FLASHLIGHTS

TEA   COFFEE   CUTTING BOARD   CHARTS

SKETCH BOOKS

SINK

NOODLES

CRACKER

BERTH CUSHION

WATER GOES IN HE

BILGE PUMP

BEANS

They pack her nooks and crannies with tools and provisions to last for weeks.

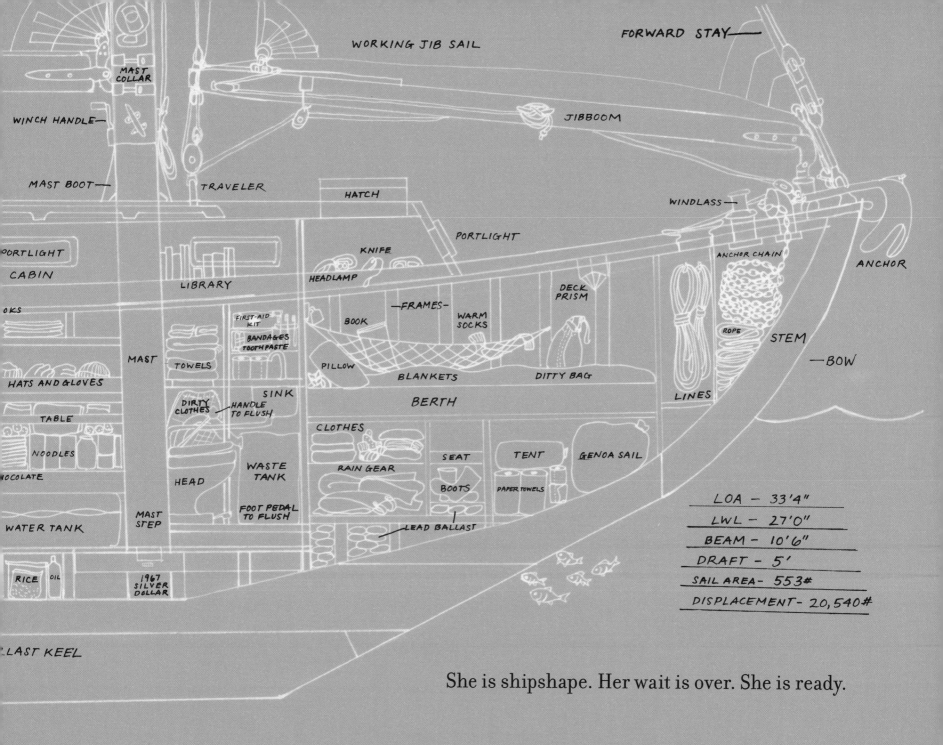

WORKING JIB SAIL

FORWARD STAY——

MAST COLLAR

WINCH HANDLE——

JIBBOOM

MAST BOOT——

TRAVELER

HATCH

WINDLASS——

PORTLIGHT

PORTLIGHT

CABIN

KNIFE

ANCHOR CHAIN

ANCHOR

HEADLAMP

LIBRARY

DECK PRISM

OKS

——FRAMES——

FIRST-AID KIT

BOOK

WARM SOCKS

ROPE

STEM

BANDAGES TOOTHPASTE

——BOW

MAST

TOWELS

PILLOW

HATS AND GLOVES

DIRTY CLOTHES

SINK

BLANKETS

DITTY BAG

LINES

HANDLE TO FLUSH

BERTH

TABLE

CLOTHES

NOODLES

HEAD

WASTE TANK

RAIN GEAR

SEAT

TENT

GENOA SAIL

HOCOLATE

BOOTS

PAPER TOWELS

FOOT PEDAL TO FLUSH

MAST STEP

LOA — 33'4"

WATER TANK

LWL — 27'0"

LEAD BALLAST

BEAM — 10'6"

DRAFT — 5'

RICE   OIL

1967 SILVER DOLLAR

SAIL AREA — 553#

DISPLACEMENT — 20,540#

LLAST KEEL

She is shipshape. Her wait is over. She is ready.

They cast off the dock lines and wave goodbye to friends and shore.

Ripples dance across the water.

They raise her mainsail and jib and ease the sheets.

Old Wood Boat leans with the wind, and water rolls away from her bow.

She races across the little green sea.

Where to?

Her family consults charts, currents,

and tides and makes notes in the logbook.

They steer through channels before eddies and whirlpools form.

Old Wood Boat gains speed with the ebb

and rides the swells with ease. With the wind abeam

and her sails full, she carries her family steadily on.

Murres scuttle aside and seals nap as she slips quietly by.
Porpoises dart and play at her bow.

They splash and squeak and then swim away.

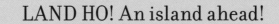

LAND HO! An island ahead!

Old Wood Boat tucks into a quiet bay.

Her family douses her sails and

sets her anchor.

They row ashore.

They clamber up the tallest peak and then slide back down.

They find scraps of the past hidden in vines and pick apples
   from weathered limbs.

Old Wood Boat swings and waits.

She was here long ago.

Her family comes back.

One swims. The others row.

They share stories and bowls of stew.

They celebrate and sing.

Nighthawks call and owls hoot. The moon rises, then the stars.

Then there is silence except for her quiet gentle creaks.

Old Wood Boat rocks her family to sleep.

They dream of wind.

They dream of waves.

They dream of islands and a sea
of green.

Old Wood Boat holds her family safe.

The moon sets.

The sea glows all around them.

Birds call. The sun rises and the wind stirs. All wake.

"Where shall we sail today in our Old Wood Boat on this little green sea?"

They raise sails.

Old Wood Boat leans with the wind.

Adventures await!

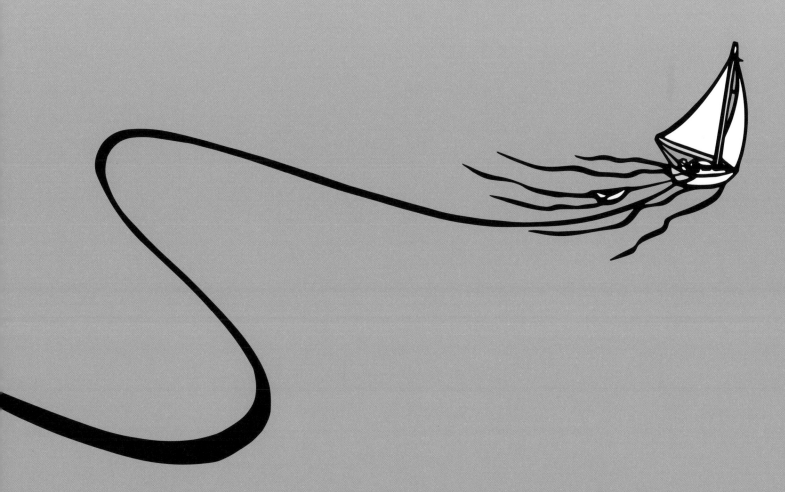

How to Talk Like a Sailor

abeam—At a right angle to the keel of the boat.

anchor—A heavy device (usually made of metal) that hooks to the sea bottom to hold a boat in place.

berth—A bed on a ship; also a cozy place for a nap.

bow—The forward part of a boat.

caulk—To fill seams with cotton or tarred fiber to make watertight.

channel—A narrow path of water between two landmasses that concentrates the flow of water and makes currents stronger.

chart—A map of a body of water that shows how deep the water is.

current—The movement of water due to tides and winds.

deck—The structures forming the horizontal surfaces of a boat; they also form a roof covering the hull.

dock line—A rope that ties a boat to a dock.

douse sail—To drop or lower the sail.

ebb—The movement of water when the current flows out into a larger body of water.

eddy—A movement of the water in an opposite direction to the main current.

gale—Strong, sustained winds of 34–47 knots (39–54 mph).

galley—Where you cook on a boat.

hull—The body of a boat above and below the water.

jib—The forward sail fixed to the bow.

keel—The strong, heavy backbone of the boat, running from bow to stern along the bottom. It helps balance the boat and keeps the boat from tipping over too far.

libations to sea spirits—The ancient ritual of pouring wine (or ginger ale) into the sea when a boat launches as an offering to the gods in exchange for safe passage.

logbook—A book in which to record details of a boat's voyage.

mainsail—The sail attached to the mast.

mast—A vertical pole that supports sails and rigging.

rigging—A system of cables and ropes supporting the mast and the sails of a boat.

sheet—A rope attached to the sail, used for adjusting the sail to catch the wind better.

shipshape—In good order.

shrouds—Cables that support the mast from side to side.

stern—The back part of a boat.

swell—A long, large crestless wave that moves across a big area of water and is made from wind far away.

watertight—Designed or constructed so that water can't get in.

Author's Note

I ALWAYS WANTED TO SAIL and would gaze dreamily at any boat. My first chance to sail was at The Evergreen State College on the *Seawulff*. The schooner *Nevermore* and her crew gave me further opportunities to explore. Thank you to these ships and crews. Thank you to A'hoi Mench and Sophie Kunka for modeling. Thank you to my nautical readers, Alex, Erik, and Alyce, and to my editorial crew of Susan Van Metre and Nancy Brennan for their bettering. Lester Stone and Jack Ehrhorn built this old wood boat and Tom and Wyndham took care of her for years. I thank them for beginning and continuing. And always, I thank my fellow crew and adventurers, Jay T. and Finn, and *Old Wood Boat* too. You keep us safe and sailing as fast as we can.

For more information about sailing, start with *The Lore of Ships* by Tre Tryckare.

For Susan and Peggy
~~~~~

First edition 2022

Library of Congress Catalog Card Number pending
ISBN 978-1-5362-1658-5

22 23 24 25 26 27 APS 10 9 8 7 6 5 4 3 2 1

Printed in Humen, Dongguan, China

This book was typeset in Filosofia.
The illustrations were created from cut black paper with color added digitally.

Candlewick Press
99 Dover Street
Somerville, Massachusetts 02144

www.candlewick.com